LUIGI AND THE LONG-NOSED SOLDIER

LUIGI AND THE

LONG-NOSED SOLDIER

BY

LOUIS SLOBODKIN

THE MACMILLAN COMPANY, NEW YORK
COLLIER—MACMILLAN LIMITED, LONDON

Library of Congress catalog card number: 63-17088. First Printing.
The Macmillan Company, New York. Collier-Macmillan Canada, Ltd., Toronto, Ontario.
Printed in the United States of America.

Luigi lived in an Italian village right near the Swiss border. And he went to school in Aroa (that was the name of his village) every day except Saturday.

On Saturday morning Luigi would get on a bus and ride across the border for a violin lesson in the little Swiss village of Biasca. Professor Tagliatini was Luigi's violin teacher. He was rather old but everyone said he was the best violin teacher for miles around.

Early every Saturday morning, after Luigi's mother packed a nice lunch for him, he got his violin case, grabbed his lunch box, and ran for the bus.

5

There were always a lot of people on the bus who were going from Italy to Switzerland. On the Italian side of the border the bus stopped. Two Italian soldiers climbed on the bus and they looked at everyone. This was to be sure there were no smugglers or prisoners escaping from Italy. (That's what Luigi thought.)

Then the soldiers wished everyone a happy journey and a good morning and they climbed off.

The bus crossed over the border to the Swiss side. Again it stopped and two Swiss soldiers climbed aboard. They too looked carefully at everyone. Sometimes they asked someone who was carrying a package what he or she had in that pack-

age. And there were times when Luigi saw people open their packages to show the soldiers what was in them.

Luigi knew the Swiss soldiers were watching out for smugglers. But they never asked him to open his lunch box or his violin case.

He often thought if he were a smuggler he could easily fill his lunch box with diamonds or some other jewels, or he might fill his violin case with gold. Then he could smuggle such treasures from Italy to Switzerland (or from Switzerland to Italy as he came home), and no one would have paid any attention to him.

Sometimes he tried to look like a smuggler. He would frown and pull his cap down over his eyes. But the soldiers on both sides of the border just smiled and patted him on the head as

7

they passed. They never asked him to open his lunch box to look for diamonds and they never looked for gold in his small violin case.

After Luigi had his violin lesson in Professor Tagliatini's house, he would eat his lunch. Luigi's mother always packed an extra cake for the Professor. Then he would go back to Italy. Again the Swiss soldiers would climb on the bus on the Swiss side of the border. And the Italian soldiers would climb on the bus on the Italian side of the border. And at last Luigi would ride home to Aroa.

That's what happened every Saturday until one Saturday when a new Italian soldier followed the two regular Italian soldiers onto the bus.

The new soldier was younger than the others. He had a rather long nose and two little, black, beady eyes. That particular morning Luigi was not pretending he was a smuggler. He wasn't thinking about anything. He had a seat in the bus behind two very stout men with big black mustaches. And he just sat in his seat looking out the window.

"What do you have in that box?" asked the new soldier in a stern voice as he came alongside Luigi's seat.

For a moment Luigi did not know that the new soldier was talking to *him* . . . Luigi!

"I have my lunch," stammered Luigi.

"And what do you have in that case?" asked the new soldier.

"My violin," answered Luigi.

"Open that box. . . . Open that case," ordered the new soldier sternly.

The two regular soldiers turned and walked back to Luigi's seat.

"Oh, we know this boy Luigi," said one of the regular soldiers. "He's all right."

10

"We can't be too careful," said the new soldier. "There's been a lot of smuggling. . . . Let's see what he's carrying. . . . Open that case, boy!"

The two stout men with the big mustaches, sitting in front of Luigi, nodded their heads vigorously.

"He's right," said one of the stout men. "You can't be too careful."

The regular soldiers shrugged their shoulders and nodded.

"Open up, boy," one of them said.

So Luigi opened his violin case.

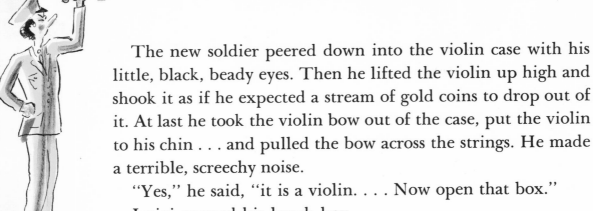

The new soldier peered down into the violin case with his little, black, beady eyes. Then he lifted the violin up high and shook it as if he expected a stream of gold coins to drop out of it. At last he took the violin bow out of the case, put the violin to his chin . . . and pulled the bow across the strings. He made a terrible, screechy noise.

"Yes," he said, "it is a violin. . . . Now open that box."

Luigi opened his lunch box.

The new soldier lifted the napkin covering the sandwiches that Luigi's mother had packed for his lunch. He poked his long nose into the box.

"M-m-m . . . Salami!" he said.

Then he lifted the napkin that covered the two cakes that Luigi's mother had baked for him and Professor Tagliatini. The soldier delicately squeezed the cakes a little. They crumbled up.

"M-m-m . . . Smugglers sometimes cook diamonds right into the middle of cakes," said the new soldier to the stout men as he licked the cake crumbs off his finger tips, "M-m-m . . . Coconut . . ."

The stout men nodded.

Then the soldier walked down the aisle of the bus still licking his finger tips. All the passengers had to open their packages for him. The two stout men had no packages.

Luigi came late for his lesson at Professor Tagliatini's house that day.

"Luigi, you are tardy," said the Professor when Luigi came in the door. "You will not be a great violinist if you do not come for lessons on time."

Luigi quickly told the Professor about the new Italian soldier at the border . . . how the new soldier had held up the bus and made all the passengers open their packages, even him . . . Luigi.

"Oh," said the Professor. "He is a new soldier — a young soldier. I do not think he will do that again. . . . Let us get on with the lesson."

15

But the new soldier did do it again. He got on the bus and looked into everyone's packages that very same day when Luigi was returning home. And Luigi had to open his violin case again. He even had to open his empty lunch box. The new soldier found some crumbs in Luigi's lunch box. He picked them up and nibbled them as he went on to look into other people's packages.

The following Saturday morning the same thing happened. Again the soldier crushed Luigi's cakes and even opened one of his sandwiches.

The same two stout men with the large mustaches were sitting across the aisle from Luigi. Again they carried no packages but nodded their heads with approval when the new soldier made Luigi open his lunch box and his violin case.

"This new soldier is beginning to try my patience," said Professor Tagliatini as he ate the broken cake that Luigi had brought for him. "Perhaps now he will stop troubling you."

But the new soldier did not stop. Every time Luigi crossed the border he had to open his lunch box and his violin case. And the new soldier found some excuse to open Luigi's sandwiches and break off a little piece, or he would take a bit of frosting from the cakes.

At last one Saturday when Luigi's mother had baked two particularly fine cakes all covered with chocolate frosting and topped by large candied cherries, the new soldier broke off pieces of both cakes as if by accident . . . and he ate up the pieces that held the candied cherries.

He mumbled as he ate the cherries.

"They might have been rubies, you know. . . . And they might have broken my teeth as I bit into them . . ."

The two stout men with the big mustaches, who again happened to be riding in the bus, nodded their heads. One of them said, "He's a very brave soldier to risk breaking his teeth on candied cherries that might have been rubies."

"This is the end," cried Professor Tagliatini when he saw the fine cakes that had been spoiled by the new soldier. "I shall ride back with you on the bus. This new soldier needs a lesson."

Professor Tagliatini prepared a large flat package wrapped in paper and got on the bus with Luigi.

They sat in the first two seats. The Professor's large flat package rested in his lap.

The Swiss soldiers at the border politely nodded and saluted the Professor and Luigi. Then when the new Italian soldier climbed up on the bus on the Italian side of the border he said to Professor Tagliatini:

"What have you there in that large package?"

"A fine big sandwich," said Professor Tagliatini clearly.

"A sandwich," the new soldier snorted. "That is a likely story. You will have to open that package."

20

Professor Tagliatini opened his package quickly and held it up close to the new soldier's long nose. His package did hold some sort of a sandwich. There were two very large slices of bread.

The new soldier lifted the top slice of bread and with his long nose took a good sniff of Professor Tagliatini's sandwich.

"Ha-Ha-A-Ker—Choo! . . . Ker—CHOO!" sneezed the new soldier. "What—What—What is it? . . . Ker-CHOW!"

"It is a sandwich," said Professor Tagliatini mildly. "It is a fine, strong pepper sandwich . . . just two slices of bread sprinkled with a lot of strong red pepper."

All the passengers and the two regular soldiers in the bus sneezed a little and smiled. Some people in the back of the bus even laughed out loud. But the two stout men with the black mustaches, who happened to be riding on the bus again, sneezed, shook their heads and tried to keep from smiling.

The new soldier was a little more polite as he asked other people on the bus to open their packages that Saturday.

But the following week when the bus stopped on the Italian side of the border the new soldier climbed aboard and he was as unpleasant as ever. He made Luigi open his violin case and he peeked in at Luigi's lunch. (Fortunately, he did not like the jelly sandwiches Luigi carried that day.)

But he did crumble up the large, sugared, raisin cakes that were in the lunch box.

"We must give that young soldier another lesson," said Professor Tagliatini. "I shall ride home again with you today."

After the violin lesson Professor Tagliatini went out into his garden and returned with something packed in a rather large cardboard box.

"Very well, we are now ready to give that young soldier another lesson," he said.

Luigi and the Professor climbed aboard the bus when it came along. The two fat men with the big black mustaches sat in the first seats and the Professor and Luigi sat in back of them. And after the bus had crossed the border into Italy, the bus stopped as usual.

The young soldier climbed aboard. He passed the two fat men because they again carried no packages.

"What do you have in that big box?" said the young soldier to Professor Tagliatini.

"A pillow," said Professor Tagliatini.

"A pillow!" cried the young soldier, scornfully. "Well, that is a likely story! Open it up. Open it up!"

Professor Tagliatini opened the cover of the box only half-way.

The young soldier impatiently thrust his hand into the box as he said:

"Let me see about that pillow . . ."

"Ow—Ow—OUCH!" he shouted as he jumped back.

"I forgot to tell you it is a thistle pillow," said Professor Tagliatini gently.

Many of the thistles stuck to the young soldier's fingers as he
hastily withdrew his hand from the box.

He frowned and plucked the thistles out of his fingers as he went through the bus quietly asking other passengers to open their packages. The passengers had laughed when the young soldier was surprised by the thistle pillow. They were still chuckling as they cheerfully opened their packages.

But that second lesson did not change the young soldier's behavior. And on the very next Saturday he again ordered Luigi to open his violin case and to open his lunch box. And of course he opened the sandwiches Luigi's mother had prepared . . . and at last he dropped the cakes out of the lunch box.

That Saturday morning Professor Tagliatini was very angry.

"This has gone far enough," he said, grimly. "We will give this young soldier one final lesson."

Professor Tagliatini prepared another package.

It was a small package and he carried it onto the bus and held it covered by his hand as he and Luigi sat in one of the last rows of seats.

The fat men with the large mustaches were sitting in the first row of seats. As usual, they carried no packages. They looked fatter than ever that day.

When the bus stopped on the Italian side of the border, the young soldier climbed aboard. And with him were the two regular soldiers and a Captain!

All the soldiers seemed very serious as they looked at the passengers.

Luigi thought there must be something very important about to happen because the Captain had never climbed on the bus before. He always sat at his desk in the little building near the border. Luigi often saw him through the large windows of the building. He always looked out of the window as the bus came along—or he sat signing papers.

All the other passengers thought this was a very important occasion too. They whispered together.

The Captain raised his hand for silence. Then he spoke:

"Ladies and gentlemen. . . . We have some very sad news. We have learned that smugglers have been carrying valuable

things across the border. We are searching for the smugglers. Please be patient."

Then the soldiers walked through the bus questioning the passengers. All the passengers had to open any packages that they carried . . . even the smallest packages.

When they came to Luigi sitting with Professor Tagliatini the Captain smiled, touched the peak of his cap and nodded at them. He was about to pass them by when the young soldier called out.

"Here—these two are carrying packages too. . . . Perhaps they are the . . ."

"These two?" interrupted the Captain. "You mean Professor Tagliatini—the greatest musician in this part of the world—and little Luigi, his pupil? . . . I know these two. They are not the people we seek."

"But—But—They carry packages," insisted the young soldier.

"Very well . . . Very well," said the Captain impatiently. "You question them."

"What have you in those packages?" the young soldier said sternly to the Professor and Luigi.

"Luigi, here, has his little violin in this case and he holds, too, an empty lunch box," said the Professor gently.

"And you—what do you carry in that small package that you hide in your hand?" asked the soldier suspiciously. "It's just big enough to carry something very, very valuable . . ."

"Oh, it is just a little something to take care of unwelcome pests," said the Professor.

"What was that? Open it up. Let's have no more talk," snapped the young soldier.

"It is of little value," said the Professor. "Are you sure you want me to open it?"

"Yes—Yes. . . . Open it up at once!" growled the young soldier. "I will look into it."

All the soldiers gathered around the Professor. He took the lid off his little package and held it up close to the young soldier's face.

The young soldier poked his long nose into the package— and then—

SNAP! There was a noise from the box!

"WOW!" howled the young soldier.

He pulled his long nose out of the box.

A little spring mousetrap was clamped to his long nose!

"WOW! . . . WOW!" he howled as he dashed up and down the aisle of the bus.

"Ha—Ha—Ha . . ." laughed the soldiers.

"Ha—Ha—Ha . . ." laughed the passengers.

"Ha—Ha—Ha—Ha," laughed the two stout men with the

big black mustaches, and they laughed louder than anyone else.

They had got up from their seats in the front of the bus to look as the Professor opened the little package. And now they laughed so much that they shook all over. They laughed until tears streamed down their faces at the young soldier dancing and howling up and down the aisle.

They laughed so hard that, one by one, the buttons popped off their tightly buttoned coats!

And they kept on laughing so hard that they blew their big black mustaches right off their faces!

Now amazing things began to happen!

Watches! All sorts of watches rained down all around the two fat men.

There were wrist watches, pocket watches, large watches, small watches, gold watches, silver watches—all sorts of watches came pouring out of the fat men!

And now it appeared they were not really fat men at all!

They had filled the inner pockets and linings of their coats with thousands of watches. And because they had laughed so hard that they burst their buttons—out poured the watches!

And as they stood there with their empty coats sagging around them, anyone could see they were not really fat men at all! They were really thin men!

And they had been wearing false black mustaches!

"It is Roberto the Robber—and Giuseppe the Gyp!" shouted the Captain. "They are the smugglers—There they stand!"

The two ex-fat men (without their false mustaches) tried to run. But the piles of watches around their feet held them back. At last they freed themselves and ran from the bus with watches of all sorts trailing after them.

"After them at once!" shouted the Captain. "Arrest them!"

The two regular soldiers ran after the ex-fat men. The men ran toward the Swiss border with watches still dropping in a stream from their clothes.

And just as the ex-fat men stepped on the borderline the Swiss soldiers stepped forward with their guns. The regular Italian soldiers ran up and grasped the collars of the smugglers. And they promptly marched them back into Italy.

"Well done!" shouted the Captain from the bus door. "At last we have captured Giuseppe the Gyp and Roberto the Robber."

And then he said, "Now thanks to you, Professor Tagliatini, and little Luigi, we have captured the smugglers we have been trying to uncover for a long time.

"And as for you," he went on, turning to the young soldier who had finally managed to get the little mousetrap off his big nose, "you gather up those watches and come with me."

The young soldier, his long nose red and swollen, crawled along the bus floor and gathered up the watches. Then he sheepishly followed the Captain out of the bus.

And from then on the new young soldier never got on any bus that stopped on the Italian side of the border.

As Luigi went to Switzerland for his violin lesson on Saturday mornings, he sometimes saw the young soldier through the bus window. He would be washing the windows of the Captain's office. And at other times he was pulling weeds in front of the Captain's office. But he was never allowed to get on the bus. And he never made Luigi open his little violin case again, nor did he crumble up and eat the best part of the cakes Luigi's mother baked especially for him and his violin teacher, the great Professor Tagliatini.